BODY SWITCH

M.G. HIGGINS

red rhino books™

Body Switch
Clan Castles
The Code
Flyer
Fight School
The Garden Troll
Ghost Mountain
The Gift
The Hero of Crow's Crossing
I Am Underdog
Killer Flood
The Lost House
Racer
Sky Watchers
Standing by Emma
Starstruck
Stolen Treasure
The Soldier
Zombies!
Zuze and the Star

With more titles on the way ...

ISBN-13: 978-1-62250-944-7
ISBN-10: 1-62250-944-7
eBook: 978-1-63078-173-6

Printed in Guangzhou, China
NOR/1014/CA21401612

19 18 17 16 15   1 2 3 4 5

Jamie Hawk

Age: 13

Worst Part of Being Famous: can't go skateboarding when he feels like it

Secret Fear: that he is growing up too fast

Future Goal: to play Eminem in the movie version of his life

Best Quality: talented

BRIAN STARK

Age: 13

Hobby: photographing animal shapes in clouds

Favorite Food: school cafeteria meatloaf

College Goal: to major in physics at Cal Tech

Best Quality: smart

1
JAMIE

"Get up, Jamie," his dad said. "You have an interview soon. *Web Celeb* news."

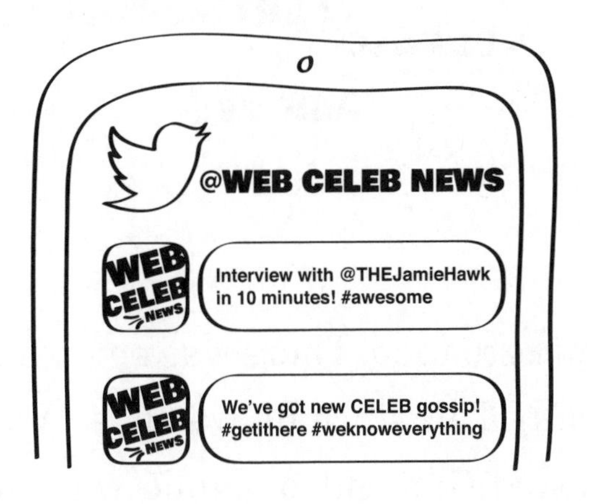

Jamie opened his eyes. His dad was staring at his tablet. Jamie hated that thing. It always meant work.

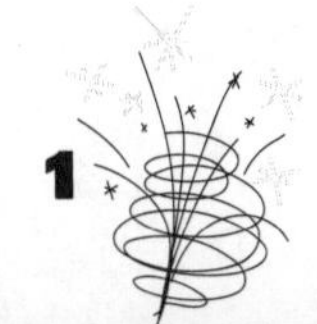

“Why so early?” Jamie asked. “I was out late.”

“Sorry. Can’t be helped.” His dad sighed. Patted Jamie’s arm. “Three more cities. Six more concerts. Then you can take a break.”

Jamie groaned. There was never a break. Not really. Not since he was five. When his dad posted that video. Jamie was singing. Wearing his jammies. Using a wooden spoon as his mic. It went viral. It happened in a flash. Normal kid to rock star.

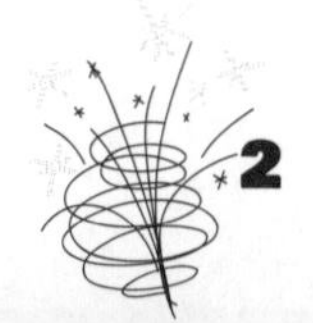

It was fun. At first. Now? Not so much.

But Jamie had his fans to think of. He didn't want to let them down. He rolled out of bed. Dressed.

His dad's phone rang. He answered it with, "What? Are you kidding? I'll be right down." He clicked off. "Problem with the hotel bill," he said to Jamie. "I have to take care of it. Stay here."

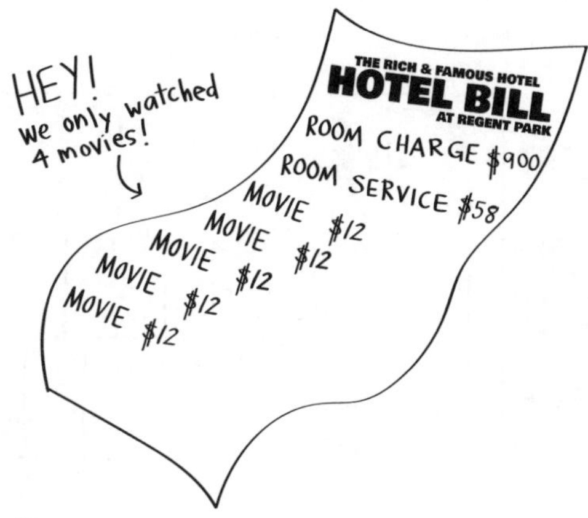

"Fine."

His dad rushed out.

Jamie stared out the window. It was a

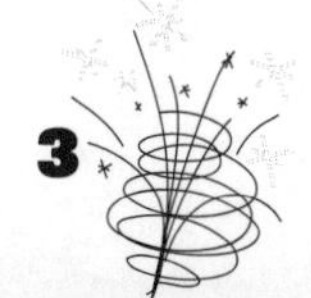

nice day. Sunny. Bright blue sky. All he'd seen were hotels. Concert halls. For five long months. He was sick of it.

He could not stay in this room. Not for one more second.

He didn't think about it. He bolted. Jumped in the elevator. Snuck through the hotel lobby. Slinked by his dad at the main desk.

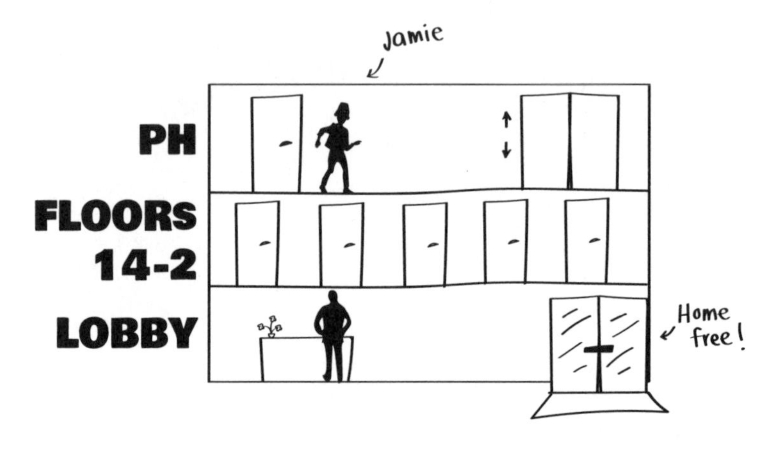

He stepped onto the sidewalk. What a relief. It felt good to stretch his legs. Get

some air. He'd be back before his dad could get too mad.

A guy with a camera saw him. "Hey! Jamie!" he yelled. "How's it going?" His camera clicked away. Shooting hundreds of photos.

Great. Those guys were always waiting. They were like vultures. Jamie walked faster. Looked over his shoulder. Now there were two of them.

Normal day. At least 5 vultures.

"Jamie!" one of them called. "Where you headed?"

Argh!

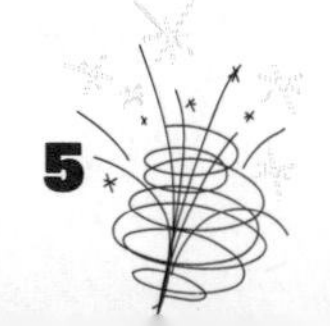

Jamie ran a few blocks. Spotted a narrow alley. Slipped into it.

He leaned against a wall. Stayed still. The guys rushed by. Didn't see him.

Phew.

Jamie glanced down the small street. It was a dead end. Most city alleys were dirty. Filled with trash. But this one was paved with bricks. Lined with potted plants. Twinkling lights swung overhead. A fountain trickled water. It was tidy. And calm.

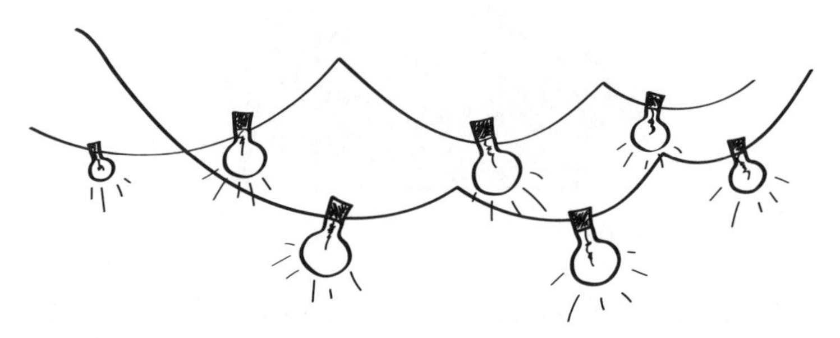

It was like the city had vanished. He let out a breath. Relaxed his shoulders.

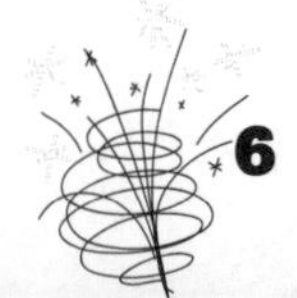

There was a blue door at the end of the alley. A sign with gold letters read Zeus's Greek Food. A huge statue guarded the door. Zeus? Probably.

He hadn't eaten breakfast. He was really hungry.

Greek? Whatever. Sounded as good as anything.

2
BRIAN

Brian Stark and his family were lost. They'd visited the art museum. Walked back to the street. Then somehow ended up here. In front of this alley.

"Huh." Mr. Stark rubbed the back of his

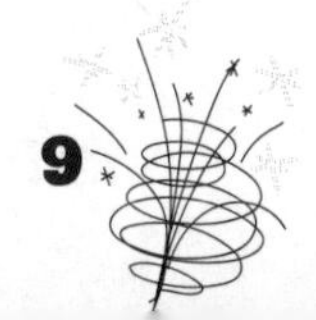

neck. Looked at the map again. "The war memorial should be here. Right where we're standing."

"Except it's not," Mrs. Stark said.

"Da-ad," Missy whined. She was Brian's little sister. "I'm hungry. My feet hurt."

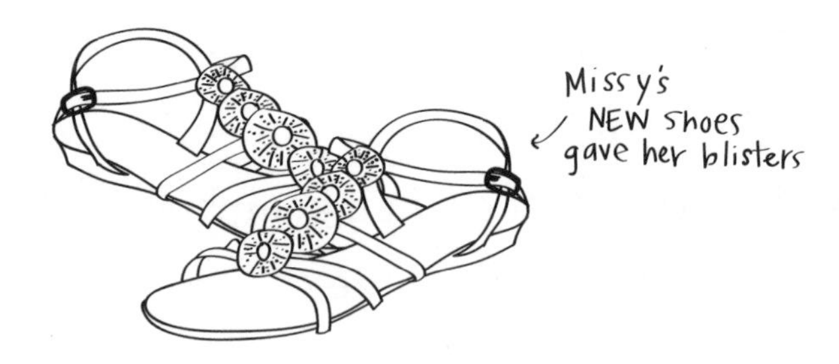

Brian was hungry too. And tired. He glanced down the alley. "Hey. There's food."

They all looked. The alley was a dead end. And there it was.

"Greek?" his dad said.

"Let's try it," his mom said. "We need food. And a break."

They walked in. There were some tables.

White tablecloths. Gold lamps. They were the only customers.

A beaded curtain swished. A man in a white jacket came out. Smiled. Stood straight. His blue eyes met Brian's. Brian shivered. It was like the guy looked right through him.

"Sit wherever you wish," he said.

They took a table against a wall. Studied their menus. Brian knew what he wanted. He tapped the table. Waited for his family.

He wasn't looking forward to going home. He had school the next day. A history test to study for. His life was so boring.

Watching Missy. Chores. Brian wished his family would take a real vacation. Not just drive into the city. He wanted to do cool things. See new places.

The man returned. Was he the waiter? Yes. He took their orders. The bell over the door chimed.

Brian glanced over.

He looked again.

Wait. Was that?

Nah. Couldn't be.

Their waiter smiled at the boy. "Sit wherever you wish."

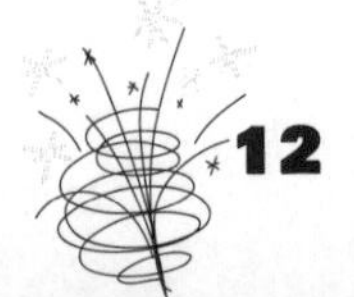

“Thanks.” The kid took a table against the other wall. Read his menu.

“Brian,” his mom said. “Don’t stare. It’s rude.”

“I think that’s Jamie Hawk,” he said.

“No way!” Now Missy stared.

It must be him, Brian thought. His friend Skye had mentioned it. Jamie was doing concerts here. At the arena. Skye had wanted to get tickets.

“Who’s Jamie Hawk?” his dad asked.

"Just the biggest pop star ever," Missy said.

"Oh." Mr. Stark glanced across the room. "Looks about your age, Brian. Maybe thirteen. He's eating alone? Where are his parents?"

"How sad," Mrs. Stark said.

"It's not sad," Brian said. "It's awesome! He's famous. He gets to travel all over the world. Do his own thing."

Brian pulled out his phone. Snuck a photo of Jamie. He'd text it to Skye. She'd freak.

The waiter brought their food. Brian ate. But all he could think about was Jamie Hawk.

He was eating lunch with Jamie Hawk!

3
THE ORACLE

Jamie peeked over his menu. That family was staring at him. Mostly the kid. The one who just snapped his picture.

He ordered his meal. The waiter gave him a strange crooked smile. What was *that* about? Jamie brushed it off. He was just glad to be out of that hotel room. On his own. Without his bossy dad. Without creeps taking his picture. He sat back in his chair.

Free time. It felt strange. Maybe he'd send a tweet to his fans. He patted his pockets. Oops. He'd left his phone at the hotel. At least he had his wallet. He could pay for lunch.

He tapped his leg. Why had he thought of tweeting his fans? Instead of calling or texting someone? Because who would he call or text? He didn't have any friends. Not

real friends. Just his dad. Members of his band. He glanced at the kid with his family. Jamie bet that kid had tons of friends.

The waiter delivered the family's food. Jamie guessed he and the boy were about the same age. What was his life like? For sure he went to school. Jamie had never been to school. Only tutors.

Maybe the kid played a sport. Was he popular? Did he have a girlfriend? Jamie bet they ate dinner together every night. His mom baked him cookies. Greeted him with a hug after school. He and his dad played catch. Tossed a football in the yard.

The kid smiled at Jamie. Jamie smiled back. Shrugged. The waiter set Jamie's meal in front of him. He dug in. The food was good. Really good. He quickly cleaned his plate.

The waiter came out. "Tell the oracle," he said.

"Huh?"

"Your fortune. Your deepest wish. Tell the oracle," the waiter said.

"Um, no thanks."

What is he talking about? He laughed to himself. *My deepest wish?* he thought. *To be normal. Like that kid over there. I want to be that kid. I want his life.*

Brian knew it was rude. But he kept staring at Jamie Hawk. Their eyes met. Jamie smiled. And shrugged!

Holy crud.

What's his life like? Brian wondered. Jamie was only thirteen. But he was already worth millions. He could live anywhere. Have anything he wanted. He sang in front of adoring fans. All over the world. Made awesome albums. He was a somebody. Not a nobody. Like Brian. Jamie Hawk didn't have to go to school. Or do chores. Or watch a kid sister.

The waiter arrived. Pointed at Brian. "Tell the oracle."

"What?" Brian asked.

"Your fortune. Your deepest wish. Tell the oracle," the waiter said.

"Thanks. Not today," Brian's dad said. "We've got to get home."

The waiter disappeared behind the beads.

My deepest wish? Brian thought. *To be Jamie Hawk. I want his life.*

Brian knew it was silly. Stupid even.

But he wished it again. *I wish I was Jamie Hawk.*

All at once his arms tingled. His head spun. His stomach churned.

He jumped up. He was going to be sick.

4
BIG SWITCH

"Brian?" his mom said. "What's wrong?"

The sick feeling quickly passed. Brian shook his head. "Nothing. Just dizzy for a second."

A chair scraped. Across the room Jamie Hawk jumped up. Held his stomach. Then

he dropped his hand. Shook his head.

Weird, Brian thought.

"We better go." Brian's dad rose from the table. "Where's that waiter? I'd like to pay our bill."

"I'll see if I can find him," Jamie offered.

Brian's heart thumped. *Jamie Hawk just talked to my dad!*

Jamie stepped through the beaded curtain. Came back a few seconds later. "No one's there. Not even a cook." He left some cash on his table. "This should cover it."

"Right." Brian's dad pulled out a few

bills. Slid them under a plate. "Okay. Let's go, gang."

They all reached the door at the same time. Brian waited for his family to leave. He didn't want to miss this chance.

"Hey, Jamie," Brian said. He and Jamie were alone. "I just want to tell you. I really like your music."

"Cool. Thanks."

"Um. Can I take a selfie with you?"

Jamie sighed. "Sure."

Brian held out his phone. He stood next to Jamie. Moved closer. Their shoulders touched.

Brian took a quick photo. Then he looked at it. It was black. What? He was sure the flash worked.

"Um. Sorry. Can we do this outside? I don't know what's wrong."

Jamie shrugged. "Sure."

They walked out of Zeus's. Both boys tripped over the small step. Both grabbed the statue. Steadied themselves.

"This should do it," said Brian.

Their shoulders touched. Brian took the photo again.

Zap! It was like a lightning bolt hitting them. Brian's head spun. The sick feeling

came back. Only a hundred times stronger. He closed his eyes. Their shoulders seemed fused together.

Then, all at once, they flew apart.

Brian stumbled. Opened his eyes. But he wasn't looking at Jamie. He was looking at … himself. How was that possible? What was happening? "You're me." Brian touched his throat. It didn't sound like his voice.

"And you're … me," said Jamie.

"The oracle," Brian said. He pointed at the statue. "I wished to be you."

"So did I. I mean. I wished to be *you*."

"You did? Why would you do that? I'm boring."

"Exactly," Jamie said. "I want to be normal."

"And I want to be famous."

Halfway down the alley, Mr. Stark said, "Come on, Brian. What's keeping you?"

"Nothing, *Dad*," Jamie said. He looked at Brian. "Are you cool with this?"

"Yeah. I think I am."

Jamie glanced at the phone still in his hand. Well, him in Brian's body. "Call me sometime. Okay?"

"Sure. Yeah." Brian smiled. "Awesome."

"Cool."

"Brian?" his dad said. "I'm sure this young man has things to do."

"Yeah, he does." Jamie winked. Gave Brian a thumbs-up. "Enjoy your stay at the Regent Park. Suite fifteen hundred. I hear it's a nice place."

"Right. Thanks."

Brian watched himself walk down the alley. Then he gazed at hands that weren't his. At clothes his parents couldn't afford.

He didn't believe in magic. But he had to believe this. Because it was right here. In front of his eyes. He was a rock star.

He was Jamie Hawk.

5
DAY ONE

Brian stepped out of the alley. Jamie had said the Regent Park. That must be a hotel. But where was it? A woman walked toward him. "Um. Excuse me," he said. "I'm looking for the Regent Park?"

Her eyes widened. She covered her mouth with her hand. "Jamie Hawk!"

He smiled. "Yes. Right. That's me.

She whipped out her phone. "Can I take your picture?"

"Oh. Sure!"

They cozied up together. Brian grinned.

By now more people had stopped. A crowd formed. A crowd! All because of him. They asked for his autograph. They took his picture. It was awesome. Like he had a million friends. But he thought he should get to the hotel.

"The Regent Park?" he asked the crowd. "Can anyone tell me where it is?"

"Sure. I'll take ya." It was a cab driver. He'd parked at the curb. Taken Brian's photo. Really Jamie's photo.

"Great. Thanks." Brian got in.

Five blocks later the cab stopped. "Here it is," the driver said.

Brian checked his wallet. It was full of twenties. Fifties. Hundreds. More money than he'd ever seen. He pulled out a twenty.

"That's okay." The cabbie held up his hand. "On the house. But can I have your autograph? For my daughter. She's a big fan."

Brian signed the back of a notepad. "Thanks a lot for the ride."

He climbed out of the cab. All at once a bunch of guys mobbed him. They all had big cameras. They took his picture. Over and over. They also shouted questions.

"Did you and your dad have a fight?"

"Are you firing him as your manager?"

"Are you dating Zoe Lane?"

"The party boy rumors. Any comment?"

Brian didn't know what they were talking about. So he said, "Um … no?" He made his way into the hotel. The doorman kept the mob outside.

Now what? Brian had been to a hotel. Exactly once. When they'd visited Grandma

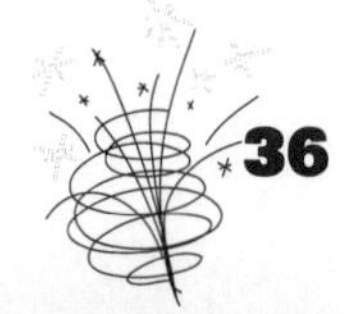

Bev. The first numbers were the same as the floor. Jamie had said fifteen hundred. He got in the elevator. The top floor was fifteen. He pressed the button.

Ding! The doors opened. He got off. Looked up and down the hallway. Strange. There were only a few doors.

He knocked on the door with 1500 on it.

A man swung it open. "There you are!" He was tall. Thin. Brown eyes. Dimpled chin. An older version of Jamie. Except for the bright red cheeks. "Where have you been?" he yelled. "You missed the interview.

You cannot sneak out like that, Jamie!" He slammed the door behind them.

"Sorry."

"You should be! I was worried. Anything can happen on the streets. Where did you go?"

"Greek food."

"I hope it was worth it."

"It was. It was great!"

Mr. Hawk eyed Brian. He grabbed a tablet. Slid his finger over the screen. "George will be here soon."

"George?"

"Yes. George. I have an errand to run. Can I trust you to stay here?"

"Sure. No problem. *Dad*."

Mr. Hawk gave Brian another look. "Are you all right?"

"I'm perfect." Brian glanced around the huge suite. "Never been better."

6
SUITE 1500

Mr. Hawk left. That gave Brian a chance to explore. This was not the Motel Ten near Grandma Bev's. There were two large bedrooms. A living room. A kitchen. A bar. A piano. A hot tub. It looked like it could hold ten people. And a massive flat-screen TV. With video games! The place was bigger than his whole house.

"Awesome!" Brian's fingers itched to grab the game remote. But first things first. He found a cell phone next to a king-size bed. Hoped the phone was Jamie's. Entered his own number.

"Brian?" Jamie answered.

"Yeah. How's it going?"

"Cool. I love your family."

"You do?" Brian scratched his head. "I need to know who George is."

"He's a songwriter. He's been working with me. On my next album." There was a long pause.

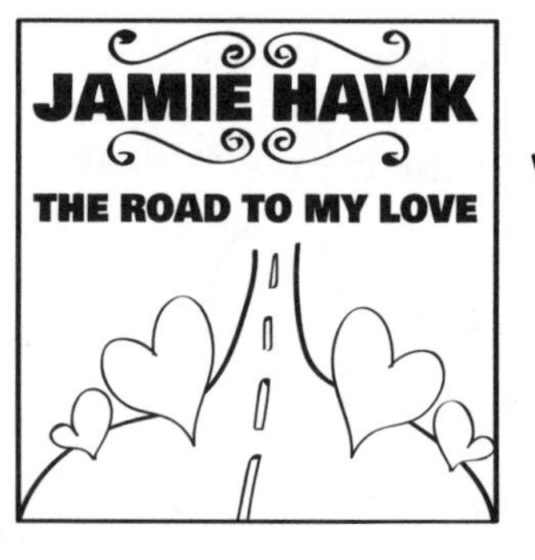

“Something wrong?” Brian asked.

“No. It’s just that I had some song ideas. I wish we shared each other’s brains. Then you’d know what I’m thinking.”

“What should I do? I don’t know a thing about music.”

“I don’t know what to tell you. I’d better go. You have a concert tomorrow night. Have fun!”

“Concert. Jamie, I just realized. I don’t know all the words to your songs!”

“Then you’d better learn them. Don’t want to disappoint those fans. All fifteen thousand of them.”

“No way! Yikes.”

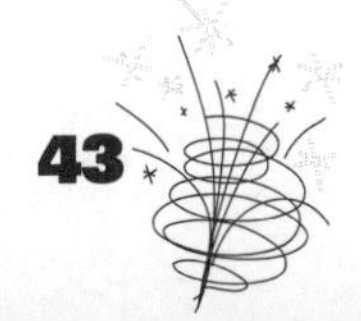

"Hey. Is Skye your girlfriend?" Jamie asked.

"No. She's just a friend. Why?"

"I was looking at her picture. On your phone. She's hot."

"Hot! No she's not. She's like my sister."

"Well, she's not like *my* sister. Time to make a move."

Brian heard voices in the background.

"Hey, really gotta go," Jamie said. "We're at a rest stop. Your fam is coming back. Loaded with snacks. Cool."

"Hey, Jamie! I just remembered. I … I

mean you … have a math club meeting on Wednesday. You have to go. Or you can't be in the math contest."

"Math contest?" Jamie laughed. "Sorry, bro. No way. I hate math. Catch ya later." His phone clicked off.

Brian gripped the phone. He'd gone to three math contests. This was the year he was going to win. He and Skye studied for it like crazy. And Jamie thought Skye was *hot*? What would she think about that?

He took a deep breath. He had to let

Skye go. Let math go. That wasn't his life anymore. He was a rock star now.

"I. Am. A. Rock star!" He punched the air.

He needed to study lyrics. But first a video game. Or maybe the hot tub.

There was a knock at the door. He opened it slowly.

A man with bushy red hair barged in. "Yo, Jamie. Ready to work?"

This must be George. "Uh. Sure." George headed to the piano. "Get your guitar. We only have a few hours."

"My guitar?" Brian said.

He didn't know how to play the guitar.

7
NORMAL

Jamie leaned his head against the car seat. Munched potato chips. He'd never felt so relaxed. Free. No concert. No screaming fans. No one wanting a piece of him.

I got his arm!   I got his leg!

And this family! They were perfect. A mom. A dad. A cute little sister. Jamie hardly ever saw his mom. His dad was his boss. He had no siblings.

Yeah, the phone call had upset him a little. He had some cool song ideas. And the thought of Brian blowing his concert? Ugh.

But so what? He wasn't Jamie Hawk anymore. He was Brian Stark.

"Stop hogging the chips," Missy said.

"Oh," Jamie said. "I thought they were mine."

"Mo-om!"

Mrs. Stark twisted in her seat. "Share, Brian."

"Sure. Here." He handed the bag to Missy. "You just had to ask."

She socked him in the arm.

"Ow. What was that for?"

"For being you."

Cute.

Mr. Stark pulled into a driveway. The house looked like all the others on the block. Small. One story. A basic square. That was fine with Jamie. His houses were so big. Mansions. He felt lost in them.

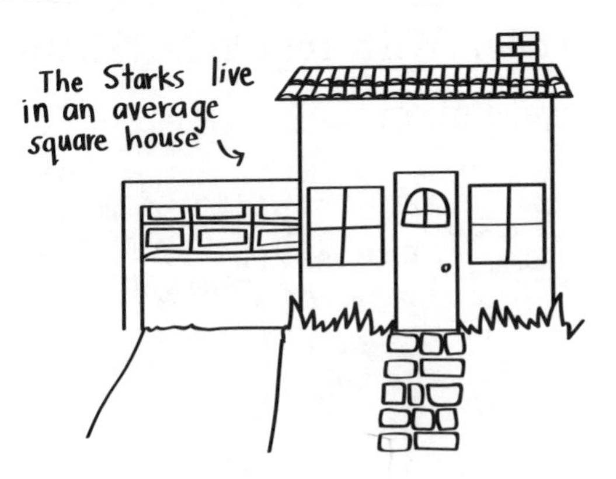

He followed Missy down a hall. She went into a pink bedroom. The next bedroom was blue. Must be his. Pink and blue. Talk about normal. He loved it.

He plopped onto the bed. Lay on his back. The walls were covered with posters. There was even one of him. Jamie snickered.

"Is your homework done?" Mr. Stark stood in the doorway. "Don't you have a history test?"

Math contests. History tests. What a drag. But he'd be going to school tomorrow. A real school. With real kids. "History," he said. "Sure. I'm on it."

"And you need to take the trash out."

Jamie sat up. "I get to take out the trash?"

"Uh ... yes."

This was so amazing. He felt a song coming on. A great song. About being normal. A normal boy. In a normal family. "I need a guitar."

"Okay. Remind me before Christmas."

"No. I mean right now."

"We don't have a guitar."

"A piano?"

Mr. Stark narrowed his eyes. "Brian. You're scaring me."

"No worries. I'm just feeling creative."

"Well. There's the little electric piano. The one Grandma Bev used to play."

Jamie jumped to his feet. "Will you help me get it? Please?"

They found the piano in the basement. Carried it to his room. Jamie plugged it in. Played a few notes. He began to sing.

His voice squeaked. It shook. Went flat. Then sharp.

He cleared his throat. Tried again. He sounded worse. Just awful!

He couldn't sing. That is, Brian couldn't sing. And Jamie was stuck with Brian's voice. "Dang." Jamie kicked the piano.

Then he thought about it. He wasn't here to sing. He'd wished to be Brian so he could be normal. Like going to school. Having real friends.

This was worth it. Totally worth it.

8
SCHOOL

Jamie got on the school bus. Walked down the aisle. Kids screamed. Laughed. An apple flew past his ear. His foot hit something. He tripped. Fell into a girl's lap.

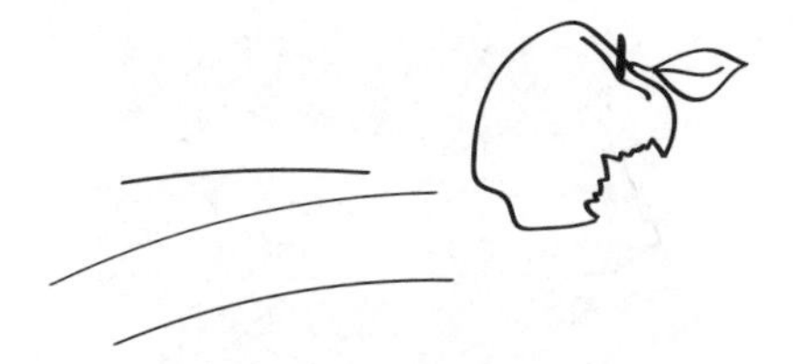

"Hey! Get off!" she yelled.

"Sorry," he mumbled.

"Dweeb!" came a voice from behind him.

Jamie turned. A kid was snorting. His big foot was stuck in the aisle.

“Ha-ha. Very funny,” Jamie said. He got up. Brushed himself off. This was crazy.

“Hey! Keep it moving!” the bus driver called.

Jamie hurried down the aisle.

“Hey, Brian!”

A girl waved at him. It was Skye. He recognized her. From the photo in Brian’s phone. He slid onto the seat. Thankful for a friendly face.

“Carlos sticks his foot out every morning,” she said. “I can’t believe you didn’t see it.”

“Guess I was distracted.”

"Thinking about the history test?" she asked.

"Uh, sure." He'd looked through Brian's backpack last night. At his books and notebook. None of it made sense. He'd figure it out today.

He stared at Skye. She wore glasses. Her hair was pulled back in a ponytail. It would look better loose. But she had smooth skin. Big brown eyes. Jamie had dated since last year. There were always girls hanging around. Before concerts. After concerts. They all wanted to be with Jamie Hawk. The rock star. Not Jamie Hawk the person.

"Why are you staring? Do I have something on my face?" She wiped her cheek.

He smiled. "No. I just think you're pretty."

"Huh?"

"Brian … I mean *I* … should have told you that before." He held her hand.

"Brian!" She pulled her hand away. "What's going on? You're acting weird."

"Weird in a good way?" He grinned.

"I don't think so." She scooted next to the window. Stared outside.

"Okay. Whatever."

The bus pulled up to Trent Middle School. Skye trotted ahead of him. Two geeky kids in the hall said, "Hi, Brian." Otherwise, Brian didn't seem to have a lot of friends.

Jamie had found a class schedule in

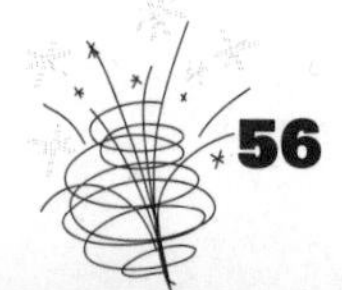

Brian's notebook. He went to his first class. Then the next. And the next. He'd never been so bored. He daydreamed. How would tonight's concert go? Would Brian blow it? Would his fans hate him?

The thought bugged Jamie. He'd spent a long time building his image. Would all that work be ruined in one night?

He went to lunch. The lunchroom was as crazy as the bus. Jamie gripped his tray. Looked around the crowded room. Skye sat nearby. She glanced away. Man. Cold.

The kids who'd said hi in the hallway waved him over.

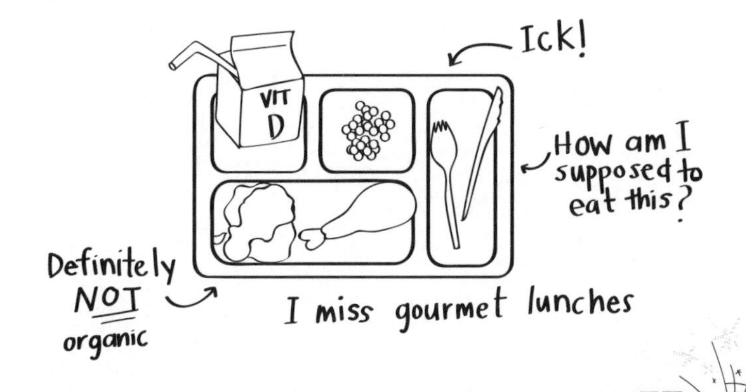

Then Jamie saw a table of cool-looking kids. Nice clothes. Nice hair. He headed their way. Set down his tray. Like he belonged there. “Hey,” he said. “What’s up?”

They looked at each other. Rolled their eyes. Moved to the other end of the table.

Wow. Middle school was brutal. Who knew?

9
ENOUGH

Brian stood offstage. The opening band was playing. They were in the middle of their set.

His whole body dripped with sweat. He'd stopped breathing a while ago. He'd never been this nervous. Even at the last math contest.

He still didn't know how to play the guitar. He'd tried to memorize the words to every Jamie Hawk song. But would he remember when he got onstage? There were thousands of fans here to see him. Him! Well, Jamie.

♫ Girl, you make my head spin.
You make my heart... ? ♫

What if he blew it? He shook his head. Of course he'd blow it. He might look like Jamie Hawk. And sound like Jamie Hawk. But he was Brian Stark. Always would be.

Mr. Hawk stood a few feet away. Swiping at his tablet.

"Um, Dad?" Brian said. "I don't feel so good. I'm gonna be sick."

"You've been saying that for the past hour."

"But it's true now."

The band ended their song. The crowd cheered.

"I mean it, Dad! Don't make me go out there. Please."

"What is wrong with you tonight? You never have stage fright."

Arms wrapped Brian in a bear hug. "Hi, sweetie." Brian twisted around. It was a girl. The prettiest girl Brian had ever seen. It was Zoe Lane. The actress. The one the photographer had asked him about.

"See if you can calm him down," Mr. Hawk said to her.

"Oh, poor baby. What's wrong?" Zoe said. "Maybe this will help." She pulled Brian's face to hers. And kissed him. On the lips! In front of his dad. Ew!

Brian pulled away. "I … I have to go.

Sorry." He ran through the back. Then out of the arena. He pulled out Jamie's phone. Called his own number.

Jamie picked up on the first ring. "Yo."

"Jamie!" Brian said. "I'm not a musician. I'm not a rock star. I don't want to be you anymore. I want to be me again."

"Huh. I don't know. I'm really digging being Brian Stark."

Brian slumped against a wall. "I was afraid of that. My life is pretty great. Isn't it?"

"No, dude. I'm joking! I hate being you. I want my life back."

"Good. Great. But how?"

"I've been thinking about it. Ever since lunch. Let's meet up where it happened. I think that weird waiter knows something. Let's see if he can reverse the spell."

“Okay. But can you hurry? Your show starts in an hour. And my house is forty-five minutes away.”

“I’ll try. Do you have my wallet?”

“Yeah.” Brian pulled it out of his pocket.

“Find the gold credit card. We’ll need it. Cabs aren’t free. Okay. Here’s what we do.”

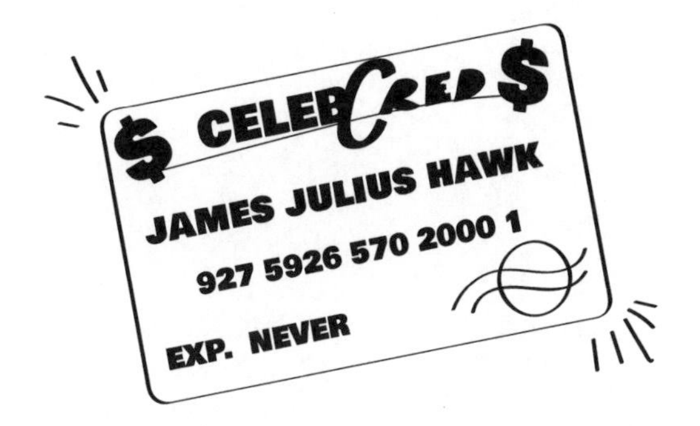

10
FINAL WISH

Brian returned backstage. He didn't want Jamie's dad to worry. Forty minutes later he snuck out again. Got in a cab.

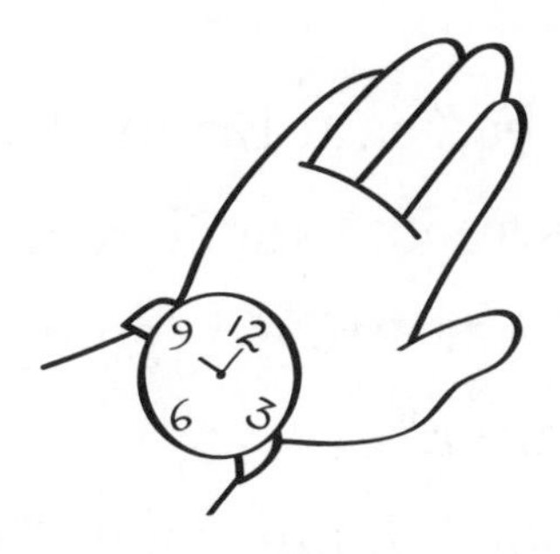

They drove a few miles. Parked behind another cab. Jamie stepped out of it. "Wait here," Jamie told both drivers.

Brian and Jamie ran down the alley.

And froze.

"Oh no," Brian said.

"What the heck?" Jamie said.

The alley was … an alley. No potted plants. No cheery fountain. The blue door was painted a dull gray. A sign on it read Acme Paper Products. The asphalt road was lined with trash bins. The statue was gone.

"This can't be the same place," Jamie said.

"It has to be," said Brian. "Those are the right cross streets. And I remember these buildings. What are we going to do? We need that waiter."

"Maybe not," Jamie said. "Think. How did it happen before?"

"The waiter. He was … odd," Brian said. "I wished to be you. Then I took that selfie."

"The flash didn't work. We bumped that

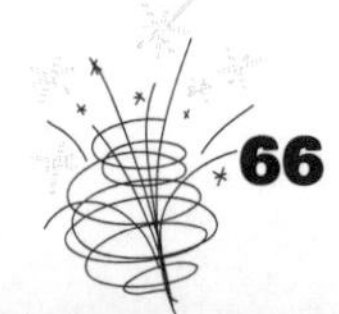

statue. Then you took another picture," Jamie said. He got Brian's phone. Scrolled through the photos.

"There!" Brian said. "There it is! That statue. Whoa. It's looking at the camera."

"But it's not here. Let's take another selfie," said Jamie. "We can wish."

"Yeah."

They stood near the door. Faced the alley. Pressed their shoulders together. Jamie held up Brian's phone.

"Are you sure you want to do this?" Brian asked.

"Totally. You?"

Brian nodded.

"Okay," Jamie said. "Now!"

Brian looked into the camera. He began to wish. He wished with all his heart to be himself again. To be Brian Stark.

Zap! It was like a lightning bolt hitting them. Brian's head spun. His shoulder seemed fused to Jamie's.

Then they flew apart.

Brian stumbled. He was afraid to look. He held out his hands. Opened his eyes.

"Hah!" he shouted. "I'm me! What a relief!"

"Cool!" Jamie said, looking at himself.

Brian looked at their selfie. No. Way. "Jamie. Look!"

Jamie sucked in his breath. "That's not possible."

The statue stared back at them. They turned. No statue. It was only in the photo.

"Hey, I'd love to talk. But I have a concert to get to. I'm about to give the show of my life. This alley gives me the creeps."

"Yeah. I know. Let's go!"

Jamie ran. Brian followed close behind.

Next to a trash bin, a pair of eyes glowed in the shadows. They watched as the boys got into their cabs. He looked like any homeless man. Down on his luck. But his crooked smile told a different story.

The next day was tough for Brian. Skye wouldn't talk to him. He wasn't sure what Jamie had said to her. So he didn't have a clue how to make things right. But it was great to have his old life back.

After school the doorbell rang. His mom

answered it. “Special delivery!” she called. “It’s for you, Brian.”

He took the envelope. “Thanks.”

Inside were two tickets. To Jamie Hawk’s last concert in the city. There was also a note.

Hey, Brian!

It was interesting being normal for a day. I don’t know how you do it! Invite Skye to the concert. Tell her you’re sorry for being a jerk. But you meant it when you said she was pretty. Thanks for everything.

Jamie

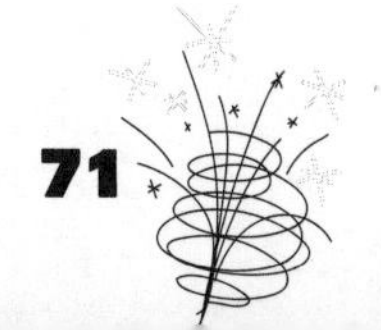

It took some fast-talking from Brian. But Skye agreed to go to the concert. They sat in the front row. Brian said exactly what Jamie had written in his note.

Skye's cheeks flushed. She smiled. Then she held his hand.